The EASTER BEAR

written by Michelle Keyes ❧ illustrated by Stella Maris

Finn looked like a bear, smelled like a bear,
and growled like a bear.

But...

Instead of catching fish, he liked hiding them.

Instead of eating honey, he liked eating chocolate.

And instead of picking berries...

... he liked painting with them.

One day, Finn's teacher asked his students,
"What do you want to be when you grow up?"

One bear said, "A fisherman because I love catching fish."
Another said, "A hunter because I love tracking things."
And another bear said,
"A beekeeper because I love eating honey."

"What about you, Finn?"
asked the teacher.

Finn knew someone else who loved hiding
things, eating chocolate, and painting.
"I want to be the Easter Bunny," said Finn.

FLORAL
VEST

EASTER
EGG

FLUFFY
TAIL

The class laughed.

"Bears can't be the Easter Bunny.
It just isn't done."

That night, Finn's parents asked about his day.
"We talked about what we want to be when we grow up," said Finn.

"And what did you say?"
asked his mother. "A fisherman?"
"A beekeeper?" asked his father.

"No, I want to be the
Easter Bunny," said Finn.

His father laughed. "Bears can't be the Easter Bunny. It just isn't done!"

"There's no rule that says The Easter Bunny has to be a bunny," said his mother. "Finn can be The Easter Bunny if he passes the test and comes in first."

The next day, Finn started training for The Easter Bunny Exam.

He had a tough job ahead of him. His sugary treats tasted too salty.

His clumsy paws made basket weaving impossible.

His egg-hiding spots were too hard.

His bushy tail twitched in a circle instead of up and down.

His nose snuffled instead
of sniffed...

... and when
he hopped, the
entire forest
shook.

But when it came to decorating Easter eggs, Finn was the best. With a few brushstrokes, he turned plain, boring eggs into something magical.

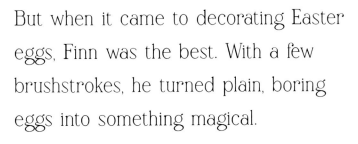

Finn practiced spring, summer, and fall until he
couldn't ignore the wind's bitter chill.
Winter had arrived. It was time to hibernate.

Finn had trouble sleeping.
He often awoke, too nervous to rest, and spent
the long winter days practicing.

One bright morning,
the snow melted,
and buds appeared on the trees.

Spring had arrived.

It was test time!

Finn felt out of place at the
Easter Egg Headquarters.

But he didn't have to
time to worry about
the bunny's stares. The
exam was about to
begin.

"Is everyone ready?" Whiskers, the Head-Eggzaminer asked. "For the first test, create a brand-new jellybean flavor."

Finn added a little of this, a lot of that, a pinch of something smelly, and a dash of something spicy. Then he poured the mixture into a jellybean mold and baked it.

The Eggzaminers sniffed Finn's jellybeans,
turned them in their paws,
then tasted them.

"Yummy," said Whiskers.
"Honey-Salmon Surprise.
Unique and delicious."

The Eggzaminers tested the contestants' tail twitching,

nose sniffing,

and hopping.

They tested their
basket-weaving

...and egg-hiding.

Finn's hard work paid off,
and he passed each test.

"For the final test, decorate one dozen Easter eggs," said Whiskers.

Finn carefully painted his eggs, making each one more beautiful than the last.

He was so focused on decorating he couldn't believe it when the Eggzaminer called: "Time's up! Bring your eggs to the judging station."

That's when a disaster happened!

Finn was in such a hurry he tripped and fell
SPLAT on top of the basket crushing his eggs to
mushy bits.

"Oh no!" cried Finn. "My eggs are ruined!"

Whiskers stood over the mess and shook her head. "I'm sorry, but without your eggs, you've failed the test."

Finn couldn't believe it. He ran away before anyone could see him cry.

"Wait," said Finn's father. "I have an idea. Follow me."

The crowd followed Finn's parents and gathered inside their den.

"Look!"

"Marvelous," said one bunny.

"Amazing," said another bunny.

"It's like being inside a giant Easter egg!"

"Finn," said Whiskers,
"With this egg-cellent example of artistry,
we declare you The Easter Bunny!"

This Easter, children may see a different looking Easter Bunny. An Easter Bunny that's more hairy than fluffy, and whose nose is larger but just as wiggly.

There might be something fishy about how delicious the candy tastes.

That's because this Easter, if you're lucky, you may catch a glimpse of Finn, the very first Easter Bear.

Made in United States
Orlando, FL
30 January 2024